The Peacock in the C
A Love Story in Thre

THE PEACOCK IN THE CHICKEN RUN

First edition. October 17, 2023.

Copyright © 2023 Dawood Ali McCallum.

ISBN: 979-8223218746

Written by Dawood Ali McCallum.

The Peacock in the Chicken Run
A Love Story in Three Acts

DAWOOD ALI MCCALLUM
Cover Art by Sophie Melissa

Dedicated to the real hero of Terminal 2

on the night of 11 December 1981
Kauser Alibhai
and to the memory of
Prita Maitra 1953-2023.
An inspiration.

Prologue

'Would all passengers for Bombay please exit the aircraft.'

Alarm bells should have rung. Suspicions been aroused. Doubts raised and rats smelt. Several frustrated travellers later claimed that they had known something was not right from the moment they spotted ground staff silently return with the two recently withdrawn wheelchairs. Not that it made any difference, because off they had all dutifully tramped. The moment the last of them stepped back into the Departure lounge around Gate 8, doors clumped shut, airlocks sealed behind them and the aircraft upon which, moments before they had finally settled themselves, slowly drew back from the gate.

'My God!' cried one horrified passenger. 'My flight!' wailed another. 'My bags!' sighed a third, who had flown more frequently.

'Sorry,' said the delegated Air France staffer, clearly not. 'You have missed your onward connection from Paris to Bombay. Hand me your tickets and boarding passes.'

'Whoa there a moment, lady!' cried Khadija Goddard as those around her, dazed by the speed with which their plans had unravelled, reached obediently for their travel documents. 'Why do you want our tickets?'

'Because we will refund your money.'

'No, no. We don't want our money back,' called out Joginder Sopal as his wheelchair was pushed through the crowd to Khadija's side. 'We want to go to Bombay. When's the next flight?'

'With seat availability, sir?' asked the staffer, savouring the twist of malice, saccharine wrapped. 'The 2nd of January.'

It was 11th December. Not only every Air France flight, but every single flight, scheduled, chartered, ABTA bonded or AITA licensed, departing any UK airport to anywhere within a thousand miles of Bombay had been massively overbooked for months. And the refunds now being offered were for their Bucket Shop tickets: hugely discounted and heavily restricted. Non-exchangeable, non-refundable, non-transferable, purchased for many hundreds of pounds less than their face value. A cracking bargain, but the refund each was now being offered back wasn't within a thousand pounds of the full fare they would have to pay for a ticket this near Christmas, even if any could be found.

Of course, as with most other things that went wrong in England that winter, it could all be put down to the weather. Even foreigners, mystified by how the English managed to find their usually pretty insipid weather of such abiding interest, worthy of repeated, detailed and lengthy analysis, had to agree that just then it justified extensive discussion. Mid-winter, just west of London was expected to be chill, dank and unremittingly miserable. Frosty dawns, damp mornings, grey, wet, horribly short afternoons disappearing into interminable, dark nights that began at 4 p.m. and stretched on till gone 8 the next morning. A dismal twilight season, briefly enlivened by the festivities of Christmas and the New Year that just had to be accepted and suffered through or, better still, escaped.

But that particular winter would go down as the big chill of '81, with the particular day on which they were booked to travel being the coldest day of the coldest December of the entire twentieth century. A fitting end to a weird year which in Britain had seen the fairy tale wedding of a virgin princess and inner cities ripped apart by vicious race riots. A year in which a Polish Pope and a film star US President were gunned down by lone crazies. A year in which the US Centers for Disease Control and Prevention noted for the first time an unusual deficiency in the immune system of five gay men in California.

A year in which anything seemed possible yet everything felt friable. A time when old certainties seemed less absolute. A time of great change. Of momentous events unfolding. Many in Britain who had started the decade as wage slaves living in rented, local authority housing would end it as salaried property owners with small but growing portfolios of shares whilst their less fortunate, fleet or able neighbours would progressively see themselves marginalised and demonised in the final, Thatcherite triumph of the burgeoning bourgeoisie.

And on the threshold of these great events, relations between the UK and India that year were defined by a rant about cricket.

How could India accept an English team which contained players with sporting links to the widely reviled and supposedly isolated apartheid South Africa? Why would England tolerate Indian objections to its choice of players? When would the winter tour be cancelled?

But on that day, it wasn't politics, race, class warfare or cricket that dominated everyone's thoughts as the mercury in thermometers shrunk like a guilty kid and barometer needles swung remorselessly towards Stormy. The temperature plunged to minus twenty-five, hiccoughed briefly then settled down, deep below zero. In homes and offices, on industrial estates and farms, power failed and pipes iced up and burst. Heavy snow fell through thick fog onto ground already frozen rock hard and stayed firmly put. Roads were blocked, schools shut down and hospitals closed their doors to all but emergencies — of which, through frostbite, hypothermia, car crashes, tree falls, skids, slips and trips there were record numbers. Normally temperate southern England was colder even than Moscow in deepest winter and at Heathrow airport, the busiest hub in the world, the proud boast of one plane landing and another taking off every minute of every day sounded decidedly hollow as whole expanses of the airfield were put out of action and incoming flights were diverted to Amsterdam, Frankfurt and Rome. Aircraft parked on stand, groaning beneath the weight of ice and snow building up on their wings, required extensive, noxious spraying and serious offloading before being declared safe to attempt take-off on the one runway all resources fought desperately to keep clear.

Hence their delay. Four hours and thirty-seven minutes. Not that much more than the running time of *Sholay*. Significantly less than that day's play in the finally settled Test series. About the time it takes an averagely fit man to run a marathon. Not that much really, in the great scheme of things. Enough however to ensure that the daily flight from Charles de Gaulle, Paris, to Sahar, Bombay, was wheels up, wings dry and first peanuts served before the London–Paris city hopper scheduled to connect with it was even cleared for take-off.

The disembarked passengers looked at one another aghast as the implications of what was happening gradually sank in. The Departure lounge at Gate 8, designed to accommodate large numbers for short times, was as chill and cavernous as an abandoned public swimming pool and just about as welcoming. They looked out miserably at the rapidly retreating plane. The barrel-scraping special of all bottom lines grimly hit even the dimmest wit: they were not going to Paris. They were not going to Bombay. They were not going anywhere. A further still moment of stunned disbelief preceded a veritable explosion of protest as others finally caught up with Khadija Goddard's reckoning and Joginder Sopal's fears. Wedding celebrations. Funeral rites. Festivals. New births to record and past anniversaries to mark. Hotel bookings. Onward flight connections. Family already awaiting their arrival in guest-houses around Bombay. These things were time specific, locked down, cash purchased and location defined. Money back? What earthly good would that be? Give up on their journeys? No way! Some shouted. Several cried. Yet more shook their heads in horror and headed for the pay phones.

And two smiled.

ACT I

I

Six Hours Earlier

'It's a sign,' muttered Duncan Goddard glumly as by torchlight he scraped snow and ice from the windscreen of his 1977 Honda Civic. 'Aye. Sure as death.'

'Bollocks.' Alex Goddard replied irritably, tackling the back window with warm, soapy water which froze as soon as it touched the glass, just as his uncle had told him it would. 'It's an aberrant meteorological phenomenon,' he added, knowing exactly how much such wordy excess would irritate his dour uncle.

The bitter cold leeched up through the soles of their boots as they worked in tandem, uncompanionably. The wind, shot through with hard snow, slashed at their cheeks, making their skin feel as thin and brittle as a shrivelled leaf. Even with mouths shrouded in thick scarves, they felt every inhalation send chill fingers reaching deep into their lungs. The older man snorted derisively on cue and wiped his ice-laden scraper against his cracked and greasy Barbour jacket. It wasn't just the casual flaunting of his nephew's extensive education that pissed him so thoroughly off: It was the verbal extravagance.

Duncan Goddard was the stereotypical Scot, through his clothes — plus fours and a deerstalker that no other countryman had been seen in south of the border for more than three decades and which had been known to cause traffic jams as tourists pulled up and whipped out cameras — and his financial prudence, which he called common sense but others dismissed simply as tight-arsed, to his carefully maintained but seldom heard West Highland accent. His attitude to language was parsimonious in the extreme. He spoke as though on a pay-as-you-go scheme that charged him by the syllable, increasingly leaving sentences, the moment his meaning was clear, for others to complete.

Duncan Goddard loathed waste, despised excess, distrusted higher education and dismissed as unmanly any labour that did not involve the practical exploitation of a manual craft. His nephew Alex's boyhood dream and early destiny had been to master the arcane craft of dry-stone walling, apprenticed to him. And there still lingered wisps of the romantic appeal of the work first kindled in Alex during summer holidays with his dour uncle in the Cotswolds. On long, glorious days of physical labour amid high, rolling pastures and big fields of short wheat and nodding fat barley. Renovating and maintaining walls along meandering lanes and beside arrow-straight Roman roads with verges ablaze with bellflower, foxglove and yarrow. Being perhaps the first to touch those stones for centuries. Feeling the craftsman's kinship with those long-dead generations of artisans who knew, just as Uncle Duncan did, the correct placement of Bee butts, lunky holes, smoots and squeeze styles.

Men had learnt these mysteries from their own fathers and had, in their turn, passed them on to their sons. Or, of course, nephews. A dying art, a specialised craft. A family tradition, albeit not one embraced by Alex's own father and forsaken too in his turn by Alex. His uncle had never forgiven him for choosing instead to go to the local Polytechnic and, even worse, study English Literature. 'What bloody use is that? Ye ken well enough how tae read books. How can three more years of *words* find ye a proper job?' he had exclaimed, in an extravagant burst of impatience and incomprehension that left him silent thereafter for several sullen days.

But it did. Both Alex and Khadija Goddard made their living from words. Checking, correcting, polishing and punctuating many thousands of other people's output every week.

As usual, neither man convinced the other and, also as usual, it fell to Khadija to break the silent but palpable tension, this time with a mug of hot Nescafe, lightly laced with dark rum. Sometimes when she and Alex were at his uncle's and the two men started sniping at each other like this she felt she should be given a blue helmet and have UN Peacekeeper stamped across the back of her jacket. It increasingly felt like policing some incomprehensible, tribal dispute. And since she and Alex had made their big decision, intrafamilial relations had gotten a whole lot worse.

Because, like hoar frost on high ground, the killing chill bit deep below the crisp and brittle surface. Alex and Duncan Goddard were not really bitching about the weather. The plans Khadija and Alex had developed, which this journey would, God willing, bring to fruition, was what really troubled his uncle, as it did with father and indeed most of both their informed but un-consulted families.

'Well,' said Duncan Goddard, handing the mug, half drained, back to Khadija. 'If you're determined tae go . . .' He opened the car door, turned the ignition key and listened to the heavily choked engine cough and grumble, as though as reluctant as he to help them on their way.

Khadija craned forward, stood on tiptoe and kissed the rough, silvery stubble on the old man's sunken cheek as the engine finally belched into life. 'Thanks, Unc Dunc,' she whispered.

A wailing, mocking caw echoed across the smallholding. Haunted, hollow and exquisitely foreign. Duncan Goddard smiled grimly.

'Yer wee pal,' he growled, glancing back towards the hen house, packed round with straw and old sacking against the cold. 'Bidding ye bide yer time.'

II

As the Goddards set off, some 80 miles to the east of them, the Sopal *barat* — wedding party — exploded into the airport.

Travel-hardened and terminal-wise, they thrust their way into the Terminal 2 Departures like a wartime convoy ploughing through choppy seas. The low-ceilinged Check-In area was thick with anxious and confused people, its tiled floor slick with moisture and stippled with muddy footprints. The warm, stale air was musty and damp as the heating, ramped up to maximum, melted the scattering of snow and ice carried in on coats, hats and bags. Light, orchestrated versions of traditional Christmas carols were regularly interrupted by tetchy, distorted Tannoy messages which echoed down and bounced around the crowd, adding to their fractious mystification. 'What did she just say?' 'I don't bleedin' know! Shut up, will you?' 'Shh. Listen . . .' 'I can't make out a word . . .'

The Sopals threw themselves into this cluttered melee with the grim assurance of old hands: stern uncles and macho nephews aggressively drove forward their well-stacked baggage carts. Moving in unison, they formed a protective phalanx within which fat aunties, pregnant wives, wailing sucklings, whining infants, mothers pushing buggies and a clutch of willowy, bored adolescents bobbed and rolled, fussed, snapped and argued, and were routinely, ineffectually bellowed at by the men around them.

And Satnam, the prospective groom and a Sopal of sorts, glumly brought up the rear. For there were no stragglers in this tight little squadron, and though the man that strode proudly at the van was Gurinder Sopal, the flag around which it formed up was that of the wheelchair-bound figure of his father, Joginder. Sitting erect, sharp-eyed and stern-voiced, issuing instructions, a broad-chested man in his very late fifties, with a neatly trimmed beard and a tightly tied red turban. He wore a sheepskin jacket, light grey trousers over legs incapable of supporting him and brown, highly polished shoes on feet that now rarely touched the ground. And he carried a box of tissues on his lap.

Jaz Sopal pushed her father's wheelchair. She glanced over her shoulder, caught Satnam's attention and eloquently glanced skywards as yet another dispute exploded about who needed to go to the toilet and why they hadn't thought of that before. Satnam, on cue, grinned.

Among the teeming thousands in Departures, theirs had probably been the shortest journey of all so far. A mere few miles along well-gritted and frequently re-salted urban thoroughfares. They were thus far less conscious of and troubled by the abominable weather. Their home, Southall, was a place where real food, fake jewellery and pirated cassettes could be had for a fraction of their cost elsewhere. Its sari emporiums, pavement traders, *paanwallahs* and *mithai* merchants celebrated and replicated — as far as weather, credit and local planning laws permitted — the mawkish glitz and hawkers' glory of the markets and bazaars of Amritsar, Chandigarh and Lahore. A place for bulk purchases from, and misplaced nostalgia for, homelands long abandoned and since transformed, in absentia, out of all recognition. A shabby nirvana that attracted hundreds every day and thousands of a weekend. Where the Sopal men, dressed summer and winter alike in big sweaters and thick jackets, ran a busy little stall in Palika Bazaar. Flogging tissue-thin and tinsel-bright salwar kameezes run up by their womenfolk in a draughty backstreet attic, copied from pictures ripped out of the latest copies of *Cine Blitz*, *Femina* and *Stardust*.

That at least was their first and remained their core business. However, they also sold other things. Almost anything, in fact. Used cars from a vacant lot off Dane Road. Reconditioned white goods: cookers, fridges and freezers. Bunches of daffodils at the gates of Highgate Cemetery at Easter. Alphonso mangoes in April. Hot chestnuts to tourists in Regents Street in autumn. And this December, holly wreaths, mistletoe and Christmas trees from lay-bys on the North Circular.

The Sopals said they were from the Punjab, called it home, and, way back in the mists, they were. But the family had arrived in the UK in ones and twos over the preceding quarter century not from India but from East Africa, following a four-generation detour to Kenya. There, like many thousand others, they had combined first railway building, then colonial service, with the setting up of numerous little general stores in small towns and distant villages to provide employment for the less capable and a steady income stream for them all in retirement. And it was to the Punjab they always turned as the source of good matches for the marriageable among them. As a result of this their current, impassioned exchange on bathroom requirements was, as were all their disputes and debates, conducted in a noisy patois of Punjabi, Hindi and English, with the odd remnant of Ki-Swahili thrown in when that was the language which best offered the *mot juste* to capture the precise meaning and mood of its speaker.

The Ki-Swahili '*Kwisha*' remained a favourite for terminating debate, particularly with Joginder Sopal. 'Complete.' 'The End.' 'Finish.' Followed, when things were really serious, by a rumbling '*Bas?*' Depending on the tone of voice, these were old words of comfort — 'there there, it's all over' — or, if spoken with a threatening, upturned interrogative at the end, statements that defied reply.

But all this voluble demonstration and verbal aggression, all this complaint, bellow, rage and threat was, they all knew deep down, nothing more than noisy bluster and hollow show. Indeed, bitch, curse and snipe though they might, and despite some quite ghastly threats of punishments which, if translated, would have sent social workers scurrying for the 'At Risk' register and alerted the police to imminent and extreme domestic violence, seldom was a hand raised in anger within this family.

Joginder Sopal, knowing too well the meaning of violence and the nature of betrayal, simply wouldn't allow it.

III

Bhao Shinde smiled as he watched the noisy progress of the Sopals. Unlike them, he travelled alone. Again unlike them, he travelled very light. He had learnt the merits of little baggage when much younger, as he travelled the hippy trail in reverse, from India up through the Middle East and Europe. Hitching rides and selling blood. Driven, like a salmon in season, thrashing ever upstream against the flow by a determination to shag himself silly. In his case, however, instincts weren't hardwired in on in some chill and gritty highland river but on the sweaty bed-sits and cheap student digs of Swinging London in the Summer of Love.

Now in his late forties, tall, distinguished, elegantly dressed, he was still good to look at and a joy to listen to. So what if he was a trifle worn and crumpled around the edges? Sophistication wears its winning. He could still boast a full head of hair, silver grey, darkening at the temples and at the nape of his neck. He had full, sensual almost feminine lips, large, dark-ringed eyes above cheeks that were rounded but not yet falling to jowls, and he spoke in a voice deepened by decades of smoking in language formed, shaped and turned by old books and good schools. Mellifluent, well modulated, gloriously toned. He appeared that day in faded jeans and a blazer over an open-necked Turnbull and Asser shirt, with a cashmere coat draped over his shoulders and a silk scarf slung with a studied nonchalance around his neck. He drifted into the Sopals' slipstream and allowed himself to be dragged along by their relentless momentum towards the Air France desks. As he did so, he wondered briefly if they were some kind of cult, a sect or perhaps a performing group. For every Sopal, male and female, old and young, sported some item of clothing, be it a turban, salwar kameez, *chunni* or tee shirt, of the same vapid yellow.

As he looked more carefully, he revised that assessment. It was not every member. It was all but the one in the wheelchair.

IV

Most people, including their respective families, wondered quite what Khadija Jafferjee and Alex Goddard ever found they had in common. Quite what it had been that had brought them together and what it was now that kept them, against all odds, a pair. Friendship, the couple would have said had they been asked, though that too had been hard tested by recent discoveries. Friends. From that first day at the Poly, when they had stood side by side in a corridor that smelt of polish, disinfectant and paint and echoed with the strident voices of overcompensating, nervous youth, staring at a notice board and trying to make sense of a timetable that used words and locations foreign to both. Lectures, seminars and tutorials sounded impossibly grown up to two freshers who, mere weeks earlier, had still been in school uniform, leaping to their feet whenever a teacher entered a classroom.

'Are you down for Existentialism and the Surrealists this term?' Khadija had asked him gravely, with what she hoped was a suitably mature academic frown on her face. He had, unhelpfully, stupidly, laughed. Nerves, not humour, had prompted the guffaw, but it was, he had recognised immediately, ill mannered, unkind and most important of all, cripplingly uncool.

'No. Gender, Imperialism and the Nineteenth Century novel,' he had said, the words tumbling out as he tried to make up ground. Silence. 'With Dr Jennings,' he had added, after a pause.

'He told us to call him Rick,' Khadija had said, enjoying the way his ears throbbed bright red. 'Well, at least that's what he told me.'

'Have you got all your books?' she had asked, still seemingly absorbed by the timetable.

He'd shaken his head.

'I'm going down to Ottershand's at lunchtime,' she'd added carefully, still not looking at him.

'Oh'

'Want to come?'

'Sure.'

Just friends.

Though her self-confidence would have indicated otherwise, she had only been in the UK a couple of weeks. She had found it a resentful, unwelcoming place in the grip of economic recession. And with every newspaper and news broadcast full of images of the arrival of the thousands of Asians expelled from Uganda, she knew most people saw her as just one more bloody Paki come to take white people's jobs and turn future generations of Britons into coffee-coloured, mongrel polyglots. Would it have mattered if she'd told them that her dad was paying out everything he'd saved for her education? That her inflated foreign student fees were subsidising working-class Brits, exactly like her to- be husband Alex, to be the first in their families to aspire to a college education?

Khadija looked at her watch but resisted the temptation to ask how much farther they had to go. Alex and Duncan Goddard stared ahead in distant silence. She thought about the peacock, calling to her from the chicken run.

Just friends.

V

If the Sopal clan had a head, the wheelchaired Joginder was it. Mentor, mediator, financier, judge and, like many who had held the post before him, the only family member not actually employed in the family business. Years earlier he had responded to one of the numerous press advertisements broadcast across the new Commonwealth from Antigua to Zambia seeking applicants to nurse in the hospitals and staff the prisons, drive the buses and clean the trains in booming, post-war Britain. Having been apprenticed in the grim Shimo la Thewa Jail up the coast from Mombasa, he had replied and, after initial training and reorientation, been appointed to Her Majesty's Prison Wandsworth.

Widely respected and much admired, Joginder Sopal was content with the easy hypocrisy of the role he, as the trailblazer and first arrival in the UK, had taken upon himself. Sternly ordering siblings to discipline their children whilst nonchalantly indulging his own. Urging the wearing of traditional clothes upon the next generation whilst, throughout the 70s, casting aside his turban, shaving off his beard and cutting his hair. Preaching against the dangers of adopting western values from a stool on the Saloon Bar of the Red Lion with a pint of mild and bitter in one hand and a steak sandwich in the other. As head of the family he had a right to say what he thought. To dictate what should happen.

No one could ever remember Joginder saying 'please' to anyone. But then leaders don't ask. They tell.

This was all taken as read and readily accepted. If, as far as his kith and kin were concerned, he had a fault — and this was not something any of them would acknowledge outside the family — it was that he too often fell prone to the Great Idea. Previous examples included a series of miserable but remarkably cheap outings in a rusty old van to grey, wet seaside resorts out of season and a near obsessive collecting of now worthless green and pink trading stamps.

The latest Great Idea, perhaps not that odd for a man who had spent his entire working life in uniform corralling ill-disciplined and resentful miscreants, was to have a range of family garments run up in the same yellow cloth. Not only did this represent good economy (a hallmark of all Great Ideas) for the material, though cheap and of reasonable quality, had failed to capture the hearts and hard cash of any customers and had proven impossible to shift even when heavily discounted, it was also a fine way to mark out and thus enable the management and control of the Sopal clan. His family members, he knew from painful past experience, were remarkably adept at getting lost at the last moment. They were almost impossible to herd through Check-In, Immigration and Boarding without someone having to make at least two mad dashes back to the toilets or duty-free shops to search frantically and furiously for some lost dreamer, blissfully indifferent to security requirements and scheduled departure times. This time, Joginder concluded, none of them would long escape his watchful gaze.

Or rather, he corrected himself wistfully, that of his son's surrogate eyes.

He felt another sneeze tickle and scrape at the back of his raw throat and tugged out a tissue from the box on his lap. He buried his face in it as the sneeze ripped up though him and exploded, muffled, wet and painful. He groaned, dabbed at his sore, cracked nostrils and sniffed noisily. He glanced around at his disparate, yellow-garbed troop, his face set in its customary warder's glower which was intended to convey a stern warning not to dawdle or wander off, but was simply, blithely, ignored by all.

His daughter Jaz leaned forward, took the used tissue from him and dropped it into a Tesco's carrier bag she carried for the purpose.

He turned as far as he was able and looked up at her neat features, seeing within them still the baby and the child and all the changing states he had cherished her through. She, amused at being so closely scrutinised, looked back down at him, one brow raised just a fraction higher, silently questioning the message behind his stare. He sniffed, and shook his head slightly. She shrugged her shoulders and looked away. A whole university of meaning within that wordless exchange.

Joginder knew his son Gurinder and many others thought her ripe and ready, indeed, long overdue for marriage. But he kept postponing what he knew his duty to be. Behind their backs he had already politely declined three quite serious proposals. Good enough boys from good enough families were not fit for his only daughter. Wait, he told Gurinder whenever the subject arose, until the right boy comes along. Someone from a good family, who could appreciate, as hers did, her true worth.

None had appeared as yet, but he was happy to wait and Jaz seemed in no particular hurry to marry.

VI

Satnam was this wedding season's prospective groom and present rearguard of the Sopal advance. Though dressed like the rest of the clan — in his case it was the turban that was yellow — looks and bearing set him apart. His features were less sharply defined and his complexion darker. Not quite as tall as most of the Sopal men but much more solidly built — characteristics he had inherited from his long dead father, an erstwhile colleague of Joginder's back in his Shimo la Thewa days. Worked there and died there too, in a situation which should never have arisen and, having arisen, should never have been allowed to get so out of hand. His widow and only child, the two-year-old Satnam, were promptly absorbed into the Sopal clan. A debt of honour and a matter of duty. Satnam had thus grown up under the relentless, impervious love of his widowed mother and the distant but eternal supervision of a sort of uncle, Joginder Sopal.

As long as Satnam could remember, Jaz Sopal had tied a *rakhi* thread on his wrist each autumn. He in return had given her things purchased for the purpose by his mother, invariably cheap rip-offs of copyrighted originals: a pseudo Tiny Tears Doll in 1968, a fake Sindy in 1974 and a year or two later, a forged and deeply psychotic looking Womble. Though she had an elder brother of her own, quiet, solitary Satnam had ever been more willing, or maybe simply more available, to be brother to her than Gurinder Sopal never was. More ready to be the one to pick her up from school. To wait for her in the van outside evening classes. To tag along with minimum grumbling on shopping trips and even, cringingly embarrassing though it invariably turned out to be, agree to be her escort and platonic date at a depressing succession of Pepsi-fuelled and tear-filled school discos.

Perhaps it was because her brother was so much older, whilst she and Satnam were much of an age. Both worked in the family business, but Satnam's duties were straightforward by comparison. Driving and delivering. Collecting the occasional debt. Enforcing the odd agreement.

Gurinder worked on the front line, day in and day out, shouting himself hoarse and trading himself silly on the draughty, overladen stall. And that was not the only difference: Gurinder was a man of big simplicities and strong opinions. Never doubtful, forever clear. Satnam had none of his clarity of view or assurance of purpose. The paths he travelled in the Sopal interest, the back doors he banged at and the lock-ups he picked up from were dimly lit, ambiguous, crowded with doubts and littered with maybes. Gurinder Sopal by contrast ducked, dived and dealt beneath neon. In a place brightly lit, where clear lines were drawn and sharp corners were very well defined.

Not that Satnam cared. His boundaries had been set for him early on by his single, immigrant parent. Work hard. Save hard. Head forever down, voice eternally low. Put neither trust nor wealth in banks. Convert every spare pound into jewellery, gemstones and gold. Valuables capable of being bundled up and stuffed into the suitcases that remained beneath their bed and on top of the only wardrobe, forever half packed, pregnant 'gainst exodus.

And for her part, though she teasingly called him Gabbar Singh, Minder and Rocky, Jaz Sopal had always thought that at heart Satnam was a great, big softie. A teddy bear, not a grizzly.

Plus, of course, there was the badminton.

VII

Alex had told Khadija about the peacock before she had made her first visit that Christmas.

In his Uncle Duncan, Alex explained with neither pride nor discomfort, the lore of the countryman — his right to graze cattle on common land and take fallen wood from wherever he found it — was taken to the edge of legal extremes and beyond. Basically, whatever took his fancy that wasn't locked up, walled in or nailed down was like to end up his. As long as it was found outdoors it was part Nature's largesse.

He did draw the line at livestock: family legend had it that not so many generations earlier a large number of Goddards had been strung up as a result of their somewhat cavalier attitude to sheep ownership. But the odd sack of cattle food here, a bale or two of someone else's straw there? Well . . .

His uncle had silently admired the peacock, perched on the crumbling wall of a local manor house, as they headed home with dry throats and cracked fingers at the end of a long summer day of walling. How the late sun set its iridescent, cobalt-blue body ablaze. It was a creature so exotic, so haughty and gorgeous Duncan Goddard knew it was destined to be his.

The next night, with Alex as nervous lookout, he had returned with a large sack into which, with the deft assurance of a man well used to handling struggling beasts, he thrust the fluttering, screeching and surprisingly strong bird. An hour later, he released it, flustered, mussed up and angry, behind his chicken wire, where, ever since, it had remained.

VIII

Jaz Sopal had started playing badminton on a Thursday after school, and Satnam had, inevitably, been the one sent to collect her. He would park up the van in the street outside and sit, with the heater running, Sunrise Radio playing Bhangra hits and a pile of Marmite sandwiches on the dash, to wait for her to finish.

One evening he had caught sight of her in his side mirror, hanging around outside and holding back the tears. All the others had paired off for matches and, with the vicious indifference to which only fifteen-year-old girls can aspire, left her, the odd one, out. So Satnam agreed to whack a shuttlecock back and forth with her for the last twenty minutes of the session, progressing from patient, almost patronising lobs through surprisingly testing rallies to a hard-fought, full stretch, court wide slog-fest which left them both panting and laughing, her the winner, eight points clear. He learnt that though he might have strength, she had speed and superb reflexes. Was as supple as willow, with amazing agility and breathtaking hand/eye coordination.

Thereafter they practised together twice a week and after nine months registered for the mixed doubles league running at the local sports centre. His *rakhi* gift to her that year had been a graphite-framed Yonex racket. Admittedly off the back of a lorry, but none the less, and for the first time, something genuine.

That had been six years earlier. Since then they had twice won the league championship, twice been runners-up and once qualified for a national competition which, due to the regional heats falling on Guru Nanak's day, they were forced, resentfully, to forfeit.

But apart from occasional tensions caused by such clashes of dates, and low level, white noise whining about the inconvenience of having them both committed to their sport several evenings a week, the Sopals were overall pretty indulgent and generally supportive of their sporting aspirations, regularly turning up mob-handed to cheer them on and running them up a range of sportswear complete with, from a distance anyway, convincing labels and logos — Nike, Adidas, Puma, Reebok, the last 'corrected' by an overzealous but well-meaning aunt who had spent many years at ESOL classes, to Re-book. Jaz had thus been the obvious choice for the sister's role at Satnam's forthcoming wedding. And it was a good match, everyone agreed, especially for him, poorly complected, vaguely parented and with profoundly limited prospects. The youngest daughter of a distant Sopal cousin, still farming in the Punjab. Homely, but a good needlewoman promising to be a fine wife, stolid worker and, God willing, fecund mother.

His own Ma, perennially wary, had gone on ahead to help his future in-laws with the innumerable last-minute arrangements. At least that's what she said. Actually, she sat hostage against potential second thoughts. Just in case.

IX

The Sopals came to a halt at the end of the queue, shushing each other, grumbling and craning forward to hear, or wobbling unsteadily on tiptoe to see, what was going on. Bhao Shinde fell into place behind them. He cleared his throat and nodded amiably to Satnam as the latter turned and, expressionless, looked him up and down.

'Bombay?' asked Bhao.

Satnam nodded. 'But nothing's going anywhere right now.'

'So I see. *Shaadi?*'

'Mine.'

'Congratulations.'

'Thanks.'

Satnam drew Bhao's attention to something behind him. A woman in a wheelchair, in her late sixties, her lined face free of any make-up, her thin, grey hair draped over with the *palav* of her stark, white sari. She kept up a steady grumble to the long-suffering ground staffer assigned to push her through the terminal who appeared studiously deaf to all moans. Over the white sari she wore a heavy Arran cardigan and a blue woollen coat. Around her legs was wrapped a tartan blanket. On her lap she held — embraced, rather — a round object about the size of a coconut, tightly bound in red cloth.

Bhao smiled down and reached out to her but then, as though thinking better of it, let his offered hand fall and stepped aside, as did Satnam. The quiet requests for access and passage from the man pushing her soon fell on less sympathetic ears. A short way ahead of them, two of Jaz's female cousins sitting, legs folded, on baggage trolleys refused to move, questioning what, as no one was going anywhere, was the point of jumping the queue? Joginder angrily spun his wheelchair around, glowered and shouted back at the unrepentant girls who pointedly ignored him. Furious, he sent his nephew Balraj to tell them to watch their mouths and allow the woman to pass. She treated him to the briefest nod of appreciation as her chair was eased past his and towards the press of sad people gathered around Check-In.

Returning from his mission, Balraj leered unpleasantly at his cousin. 'So we finally get to see Sambo married, Jaswir. Who'd have thought?'

'Don't call him that,' snapped Jaz, knowing he was just trying to wind her up and knowing she was letting him.

'Wonder if it's all that Marmite that turned him that colour?'

She aimed a kick at his ankle, which he sidestepped, laughing.

X

Alex and Khadija Goddard were still far from the airport and uncomfortably aware of how rapidly time was passing and how agonisingly slowly Duncan Goddard was driving. The little Civic struggled to stay on the icy roads, its wipers, prone to freeze to the windscreen unless kept in constant motion at top speed, fought a losing battle against spreading frost patterns and powdery, driving snow. Inside the vehicle, heater on full blast, Uncle Duncan squinted into the blizzard, his nose up close to the windscreen whilst Alex wiped away the condensation that formed on the inside of the glass.

As they headed down onto the eastbound carriageway of the M4 the motorway was barely discernible, so impenetrable was the blanketing fog. Normally heavy with vehicles racing towards London, today it presented a grim vista more reminiscent of a retreat from Moscow. They passed numerous snow-covered vehicles abandoned on the hard shoulder by drivers now trudging through ankle-deep snow to AA emergency phones, their breath steaming, collars up and shoulders rounded against the cold.

'Wireless,' the old man grunted, as he changed down to second gear. 'Travel news.'

'We'll never make it on time,' Khadija sighed.

Alex tuned the rarely used radio through wailing static to a local BBC channel. 'Doesn't sound like we need to,' he said, as the total paralysis of London Heathrow was reported, followed by a police announcement discouraging all but emergency journeys.

Uncle Duncan sighed. 'It's a . . .'

'. . . sign,' concluded Alex, turning and reaching over the seat back for Khadija's hand. 'Yes it is, sure as new life. It's a sign everything's going to be OK.'

XI

The airport re-opened for business just as Duncan Goddard, after one horrified glance at the parking charges, swerved out of the queue for the car park, across three lanes of hooting traffic, and pulled over kerbside of Terminal 2 Departures. Keeping the Civic's engine running, he bundled Alex, Khadija and their bags out onto the pavement and pulled away, without a backward glance.

'And a very merry Christmas to you too.' Alex sighed as he waved after the departing car.

'You know what he's like.' said Khadija, looking around for a baggage trolley. 'How he feels about this.'

'Weird, the peacock crying just as we were leaving.' said Alex. 'Spooky. Like a sign.'

'Don't you start,' sighed Khadija, giving up on the hope of a trolley and heaving one of their bags onto her shoulder.

'What?' asked Alex, hands spread, an image of affronted innocence.

'*It's a sign. Aye, sure as death,*' she mimicked in an exaggerated Scottish accent. 'You have no idea how like him you are sometimes. Portents. Messages. Meaning. Grab that bag and, and for fuck's sake, let's go.'

Inside the terminal, Check-In staff, moments earlier capable of little more than dumb shrugs, now leapt into action, calling forward passengers for the flights allocated first slots in the hastily recast departure schedule. It was just one more anomaly of that strange day that whilst the airport was choked with hopeful travellers, many of the planes currently on stand and clear to go looked likely to depart half empty. Terminal 2, dedicated to short-haul flights into Europe, was primarily the domain of business travellers, a significant number of whom had needed no more than a sleepy glance out of their windows that morning to be convinced of the wisdom of heeding police warnings against travel.

Fortunately, someone realised the opportunity so many no-shows offered and instructions went down to Check-In: call forward ticket holders by destination, forget about flight numbers. Thus Alex and Khadija, Bhao Shinde and the lady in the wheelchair all ended up with boarding passes for the earlier flight on which only the Sopals had originally been booked. Together they were rushed through formalities, marched past grumbling queues at Security, bustled to Departure Gate 8 and thrust unceremoniously on to the waiting plane.

Seatbelt and No Smoking signs flashed. Alerts pinged amid a cheesy piped ballad about Christmas, snow and home. Seatbelts clunked shut. A child chattered excitedly and was quietly, indulgently, ineffectually shushed by its mother. Sopal menfolk, although used to daily lugging of heavy loads, groaned, muscles trembling, as they tried to cram yet another of the capacious, weighty bags sneaked on as hand luggage into already overstuffed lockers. Satnam was called on more than once to add his muscle to their efforts to transcend the laws of dimension and volume. Joginder watched as his eldest son carried out a silent head count on his behalf — something he had, prior to this trip, always done himself. Gurinder nodded down to him — everyone on board first go. In record time too. Jaz, sitting next to her father, saw the swagger in the son and felt the trapped anger in the father, still shamed at having been carried by Satnam onto the plane and deposited into his seat. At having to ask Gurinder to do this, his final check, such a part of him and a ritual of every previous journey.

Bhao Shinde, two rows back and on the aisle, thrust his feet out beneath the seat in front of him, stretched and yawned. He looked across at his neighbours — Alex next to him, Khadija on beyond, next to the window. He nodded at them. Alex smiled back.

'Looks like we're on our way,' Bhao said, rubbing his hands together. 'Off on holiday?'

'Yes and no', said Alex.

Bhao chuckled. 'That must mean you're visiting family.'

'Perhaps', said Alex.

'Well, I'm going home, after many years and for good. First visit to India?'

'Yes'

Bhao seemed about to say something more but paused, a look of infinite sadness on his face as the white-clad old woman, still clutching the red bundle to her belly, shuffled unsteadily through the plane to her seat three rows further back. A stewardess followed immediately behind her, supporting her elbows and calling, with increasing impatience, for people *please* to make way. The woman, arched forward, moved carefully, very slowly, her face a resigned grimace of discomfort, regret and distress. Another stewardess eased herself from the rear of the plane through the crowd of people still trying to fit luggage into overhead lockers and came towards them. She reached to relieve the woman of the bundle, but it was held even tighter as the woman glared around, shaking her head vigorously.

'She's hanging on to that package like dear life,' Alex whispered. 'What do you think she's got in it?'

'Well, I don't think it's her lunch,' said Bhao, airily. 'I suspect it's more a case of who than what.'

'You mean . . .?'

'Ashes to be cast upon the welcoming breast of Ma Ganga,' said Bhao. 'He's off to his wedding,' he observed, nodding towards Satnam, a few rows ahead of them, patiently rearranging bags in the overhead lockers, 'She's off to a funeral. . .'

It was at that moment, the announcement was made:

'Would all passengers for Bombay please exit the aircraft.'

ACT II

I

Their best hope was to hold firm at Gate 8. 'As long as we are here,' Khadija told Alex, 'they can't wash their hands of us. As long as we're here they have to do something.'

The airline too was acutely aware of that fact. They were also very conscious that affordable options for resolving this impasse were as restricted as the now worthless tickets this suddenly troublesome bunch had bought. They couldn't stay where they were, though. That much was clear. They were airside. They had left the UK but had yet to get anywhere else. They were currently, quite simply, legally, nowhere. They were asked to return through Immigration and Security and await developments landside but simply refused to go.

The airline staff handed out refreshments vouchers and withdrew to contemplate their next step.

Khadija was too wound-up to think about food, so Alex headed off on her behalf. Catering airside was designed to offer light bites, sweets and Cokes for whingeing kids and a quick, ludicrously overpriced pre-boarding snifter to the confirmed drinker. Alex traded Khadija's voucher for a plastic- shrouded slab of cherry cake and a packet of cheese and onion flavoured crisps for when she did feel peckish, as inevitably she must. As he mulled over what to get for himself, Bhao Shinde appeared.

'If you want my advice, don't squander it on food,' he observed. 'Maximum calorific value comes from alcohol.'

Alex ordered whisky. 'You drinking?' he asked Bhao.

'No', Bhao replied, wistfully. 'I've rather lost my taste for it of late.'

Alex raised the plastic glass in which his drink was served to Bhao. 'Your health.'

Bhao laughed. 'Right. Happy days.'

Several of the Sopal men had also gravitated to the kiosk. Hands were shaken and hard-luck stories exchanged. Alone among this increasingly boisterous bonhomie, Satnam stood apart, silently sipping a gassy lager whilst he waited for a bulk order of Cokes and Tango Orange cans he had been delegated to fetch for the women.

'Hey, groom, not gloom,' cried Gurinder Sopal, pointing at Satnam to a chorus of laughter. 'Why the long face?'

'Cos that's the only long part of him,' declared Balraj Sopal. 'It's not true what they say about darkies.'

To emphasise his point, he measured a tiny distance on the smallest finger of his left hand between the forefinger and thumb of his right that prompted another raucous chorus of guffaws and a series of double entendres about not measuring up and being caught short on his wedding night.

Satnam looked unmoved at the harassed and short-tempered woman serving behind the counter, at the wall of barracking men around her waving their vouchers and calling out orders. He eyeballed Balraj, who met his stare, but fell silent. In turn, Satnam looked from one Sopal to another, a quiet challenge in his eyes. One by one they looked away, talking loud, pretending they hadn't noticed his silent, profoundly menacing but totally emotionless stare.

One more thing he'd learnt from his mother.

II

With the younger men crowded around the little food outlet, their seniors stood, round shouldered, grumbling whilst their wives and mothers settled noisily into the seating area near the gate. Ever prepared and deeply suspicious of in-flight food, the Sopal womenfolk had secreted amongst their many bags a whole range of snacks, tightly wrapped in BacoFoil and carefully packed in plastic ice cream cartons secured with elastic bands: samosas, meat and vegetarian pakoras, *chaat*, kebabs, *dahi wada* and even a neat pile of Marmite sandwiches for Satnam. Whilst they waited for their drinks, food was pooled and passed around. Khadija, though too stressed out to think of eating, found a paper napkin thrust in her hand, containing a range of fried titbits still warm from the oil.

Joginder Sopal thought he would self ignite if he had to endure another minute of people standing around him talking nonsense over the top of his head as though unaware he was even there. Since his injury the fundamental relationship between height, stature and authority had been made brutally clear to him. Long used to looking whoever he was speaking to square in the eyes, he struggled now with his new groin-level perspective and angled interactions, ending most days with a severely stiff neck and a splitting headache. He headed off to the only other person on his eye level, in a wheelchair, alone and also largely ignored, over by the toilets. Several Sopals, belatedly shamed, made to push him but were brusquely told to go away.

Though a shared disability and subsequent reliance on the convenience of others tendered a potential bond, Joginder, once settled next to the woman, struggled to think of anything to say. Eventually he nodded towards the cloth-wrapped urn.

'My son.' The woman stared straight ahead. 'He'd lived over here for years. It should have been my pyre that called him home. Not me, taking him, like this.'

'Sorry.' Joginder shook his head, acknowledging the injustice. 'Is there anything you need?' he asked.

'Just to get home, like everyone else.'

'Haven't you got anyone with you?'

She stroked the urn she carried, dry eyed, a bitter little smile on her face. 'Only him.' She shook herself, as though trying to slough off the grief, at least temporarily. She turned and frowned at Joginder. 'How did a strong-looking man like you end up in a wheelchair? An accident?'

'More an industrial injury,' began Joginder, happy to find something to talk about at last. 'Prison officer, see? Or used to be. Twenty-eight years all told. More, including my time in Kenya. I was already three months past retirement. Only stayed on so they could sort out how much of my time in Kenya counted towards my pension. Then, when I was on nights, there was a problem. A C and R — Control and Restraint. Should have been simple but it all went wrong.'

'There should have been three of us entered that cell. I thought there was. I should have had backup. I thought I had. Instead, I went in alone and came out and over the landing. Broke my back on the balustrade before I hit the suicide net. The next day they heard my pension was sorted.' He stopped, coughed, then cleared his throat. 'My name is Joginder.'

'Aruna,' she said. 'None of this makes any sense, does it?'

'No, Aruna-*behenji*. Once I thought it did. But no, I don't think it does.' Joginder smiled sadly, told her she just had to ask for any help she needed and wheeled himself over to where Khadija sat, still clutching her little bundle of food.

'You should eat, *beti*,' he said.

'So I keep being told.'

'So what do we do now?'

'I don't know. Start ringing newspapers? TV. *That's Life. Nationwide.* You know, get publicity. Embarrass the airline. Make someone care.'

Joginder chuckled, delighted at last to have a task to organise. He nodded, glanced around and snapped out quick instructions. Hands dived into pockets and small change was sorted through until a fat handful of 10p pieces were available for distribution. He nodded at the bank of a half-dozen payphones in the corner of the lounge. Quickly they drew up a list of targets: *The Daily Mirror, The Sun, The Daily Mail.* Capital Radio and LBC. ITV newsrooms and BBC consumer programmes. Khadija rang directory enquiries and jotted down the requisite numbers. She began to dial the first on the list but Joginder reached up and touched her wrist.

'Wait.'

He called across to a gaggle of Sopal adolescents, who loped over and lined up unenthusiastically. Joginder cleared his throat and with a groan the youths extracted their chewing gum. Several carefully rewrapped the moist, grey globule in its crumpled packaging. Others flicked theirs, with varying degrees of success, towards a nearby rubbish bin. Tegbir, to Joginder's obvious disgust, swallowed.

Jaz, too, joined the line-up. Joginder asked Khadija to prepare a brief statement each recruit could recite and despatched them to the phones with instructions that, as soon as they got through to anyone who displayed even the most distant interest they should call Khadija over. Side by side the Sopals stood, dialled and waited, priming their phones with coins. As the pile of change shrank it became apparent that their plight was not capturing the imagination of the media. News had just broken that the Queen herself, on her way to visit Princess Anne, had been cut off by waist-high snowdrifts and forced to seek refuge in a Cotswold pub. A bunch of frustrated holiday makers and grumbling foreigners stuck in Departures was way down the news agenda, so far below tales of rescued cats and stranded cattle as to drop noiselessly off the end.

III

Balraj Sopal carried a treble measure of whisky to his cousin Gurinder. '*Thaiyaji* should just let you deal with all this shit,' he said as he handed it over, nodding at the wisdom of his own words.

Gurinder sipped pensively but said nothing. Balraj interpreted that as an invitation to continue. 'Now he's retired and what with him having been crippled and all. I mean, what the fuck are we doing, all going to India for Sambo's wedding anyway? It's not like he's even part of this family.'

'Don't call my father a cripple,' growled Gurinder.

'No, no, sorry!' said Balraj, with a quick, nervous smile. 'No disrespect. You know that, man. I would never . . . Just that he needs his rest. Must do. Look, I'm just saying, if you were in charge, would we be going to this wedding, when there's serious trading to be done? That's all I'm saying.'

'My father takes his responsibilities seriously,' said Gurinder. 'So do I.'

'Course you do. No one doubts that, man. No one. But . . .' he paused, sucked in and bit on his lower lip, frowning thoughtfully and shaking his head. 'I mean, we could have shifted another couple of hundred trees before Christmas. Fuck! We could have made money! That's all I'm saying.'

'Satnam . . .' Gurinder began.

'Isn't one of us, no matter how hard he tries.'

'What?'

'Well, shit man! Look at the way he's always hanging round Jaz. I mean, I'm not saying anything about your sister,' he rushed on, picking up the dangerous glint in Gurinder's eyes, and holding up both hands in surrender. 'She's like a little sister to me too. You know that. I love her to bits. That's why it pisses me off seeing him always hanging around her. I mean, what the fuck?'

IV

Bhao, standing with his back to the kiosk and looking out over the snow-covered airfield, turned as Alex passed him. 'I hate snow,' he mused, 'or rather, I despise and I pity it.'

Alex turned, starting slightly. He had not even been aware Bhao was there. 'I'm sorry?'

Bhao nodded towards the paralysed airport. 'Rain is tireless, industrious, opportunistic. It seeks out the tiniest crack and works away at it. It exploits wind, uses gravity and takes advantage of frost to shape and change whatever it touches — and my, is it patient! Percolating, trickling, dripping, seeping. Over centuries shattering mountains and scouring out caverns twice the size of cathedrals. Slowly, quietly, deep down, in the dark.'

'And snow?' asked Alex, amused.

'Is rain's mute and stupid brother. It just tumbles dumbly down and lays there. Rain drives. Snow merely drifts.'

'It can look good.'

'Only at first. Like an idiot child prepared for an outing, it can start out fresh and clean. But does it stay that way? It soon gets dirty and turns to slushy muck. You can plough it and you can dig it, but it is sterile. Infertile. It creates nothing.'

'Snowmen? Snowballs?'

'Precisely. It contributes nothing of lasting value yet stands accused of much. Take right now. Watch the news. Read the papers. *Snow grips Britain. Snow cuts blood supply to hospitals.* What nonsense! Frost is the true criminal here, with wind its henchman and ice its hired gun. But who is it that hangs around and takes the blame? Poor, dumb, gullible snow. Who needs it?'

'Penguins and polar bears?'

'I don't think so! You see them in concrete enclosures in zoos the world over. Sure they look disoriented and miserable, but that's just first-generation displacement. Immigrant blues. Would you want to walk miles on frozen feet or dig through metres of snow for your food when you can have it handed to you on a plate? Later generations will thank them, believe me.'

'They say eskimos have twenty-eight different words for snow.'

'I seriously doubt that. But even if they do, they probably have twenty-eight different words for crap too. And they're probably the exact same ones.'

Bhao glanced around at the increasingly noisy Sopals. His face, devoid now of humour, looked much older, lined and tired. 'Don't be snow, is all I'm saying,' he whispered, as though to himself. 'No man should ever be snow.'

V

Khadija sat down beside Jaz: they had worked together on the failed phone campaign and already shared grumbles about the situation they were in. She stretched her arms along the back of the seat and rolled her head to ease the stiffening she felt spreading across her shoulders. As she raised one hand, a button on the cuff of her sleeve caught between the armrest and the back of the bench on which she sat and went spinning across the floor.

'Oh, bollocks, shit and buggeration!' she groaned, reaching down for it, but Jaz beat her to it, kneeling to reach beneath the bench.

'Thanks', said Khadija as Jaz, still kneeling at her side, handed the button to her.

Jaz smiled and sat beside her. 'No sweat. Want it stitched back on?'

'Can you?'

Jaz exaggeratedly let her jaw drop as though stunned by such a dumb question. She delved into the deep pocket of her track bottoms and hauled out a small sewing kit whilst Khadija slipped the heavy jacket off.

'It won't be a perfect match,' she warned as she deftly threaded a needle, knotted off the cotton and reached for the sleeve.

Khadija wrapped her scarf around her and shivered at the chill, 'As my mother would say, you'll make someone a fine wife.'

Jaz rolled her eyes. 'Don't.'

'So I'm guessing this isn't your wedding party?'

Jaz shook her head. 'My...well, he's kind of a cousin/brother. He's gaining a partner. I'm losing one.'

Khadija frowned her incomprehension.

'Me and him. We play badminton. Mixed doubles.'

'Well, surely that doesn't have to end simply because one of you is getting married? Look at . . . Torvill and Dean! Ice dancing all over the world. She with her legs wrapped around his neck half the time and him constantly grabbing her bum! They're partners but they're not a couple.'

'Yeah, well, they're not Sopals. They're not even Sikhs.'

'That would be hard to deny. Poor things. Probably why they do it in the first place.'

Jaz raised the sleeve with its newly replaced button firmly attached to her lips and bit through the cotton. She handed the jacket back to Khadija. 'There we go.'

'Thanks,' said Khadija as she slipped the jacket back on. 'That's brilliant.'

'Child's play.' Jaz nodded around at her. 'Any of us could have done it. You're sitting with the most powerful set of sewers in Southall.'

They sat together in silence for a moment.

'What do you do?' Jaz asked.

'Me? I'm a proofreader.'

'A what?'

'A proofreader. My husband too. We work for a publishing house that specialises in academic texts.'

'Sounds . . . great. First trip to India?' Jaz asked.

'Hmm. You?'

'No, we go every year or so. Family stuff, like this. Are you visiting relatives?' asked Jaz.

'Time will tell,' said Khadija obscurely. 'I don't have family in India. My folks are all in Tanzania now. Or Canada. Or here. We're going to adopt a child,' she added, unsure quite why.

'Wow! Congratulations!'

'Let's not tempt fate. There's still a lot to sort out . . .'

'Got photos?'

'Just the one.' Unzipping her bag, Khadija took out a black-and-white passport snap. Jaz studied the image. A round face, features and structure still in the process of forming. A tiny chin, a little mouth, slightly open, cute ears and an untidy fuzz of hair. Surprisingly elegant eyebrows that seemed better fitted to an older faced and a large tilak centred on the forehead. Widely set eyes that stared out, deeply uncertain, as though uncomfortable or unhappy with being held still for the studio image, as was evidenced by the bunching of the patterned frock up under her throat and the large hand across her chest. As though aware, too, that the taking of this photo presaged profound change, far beyond her ken, control or imagination. 'She's four months old. In an orphanage in Bombay.'

'She looks sweet,' said Jaz, handing the photo back.

Khadija regarded the image as though seeing it for the first time. 'Does she? I must have looked at this picture a thousand times. Stared at it for hours. Kept it stuck on the fridge in our flat. I keep hoping to find . . . oh, I don't know . . . a connection of some kind. Our next door neighbour says she can see that this little one's been here before. Says it's in the eyes. But the more I look, the less I see . . . anything.'

'You'll know when you hold her,' said Aruna, having slowly propelled herself across the lounge. Both the younger women turned to look at her. 'May I see?' she asked.

Khadija handed the picture over. 'She's just waiting,' the older woman concluded. 'Waiting for a mother to take her home. You can see *that* in her eyes. What's her name?'

'Nutan, on the paperwork.' said Khadija. 'But we can change that when we adopt her. We'll have to, as we'll bring her up as a Muslim.'

'What will you call her?' Aruna asked, returning the picture with a certain reluctance.

Khadija sighed and looked around. Over by the vast glass wall looking out across the now still and misty runway, a clutch of young mothers, fresh faced and inordinately confident, walked up and down, shifted dozing sucklings from one hip to the other. They cooed, clucked and glowed, smug as corrupted priests, and Khadija felt a visceral envy.

'We haven't decided,' she snapped, thrusting the photo back into her bag. She wished she had never mentioned the purpose of their trip. She felt exposed, unfairly challenged and extremely angry.

The older woman sniffed. 'No one's real until you say their name.'

VI

At quarter past four, the day beyond the glass wall began to fade and lights, glowing pale amber and dull yellow, stood out ever more clearly. In the gloaming planes, vehicles, then buildings progressively lost their definition. Signs blurred, dimensions merged and a sense of melancholy timelessness pervaded the terminal. Was it mere hours they had been there? It seemed like years. It could have been forever.

Gurinder had been dully mulling over Balraj's words. It *was* time he took responsibility. He couldn't forever remain his father's eyes and voice. It was time for him to act on his own authority. No one was better placed to do so. Everybody knew that. And it wasn't simply his right, it was his duty. His father had done his part, and, no one could deny, done his best, but his days were now gone. He was old. He was tired. And let's face it, he was, though Gurinder felt bad even thinking the word, now crippled. Anyway, even when he'd been fit and strong he'd never really understood life here. Not as Gurinder did. Sure, he could hear the barracking, the shout and barter, and see the bustle and fuss of Palika Bazaar. But he could never really feel its click, beat and thrum. Take its pulse in an instant and just know where the drops would work and the bungs would pay.

Because Joginder still believed in respecting traditions that even his white neighbours now blithely ignored. Obeyed rules and followed codes others were sure no longer applied to them. He was, and always would be, the visitor here. Polite, courteous, careful. No matter how many years he stayed. Whilst Gurinder was at home. Hardwired into the life of the place.

Gurinder looked at his father. How drained, he suddenly realised, how worn, how shrunken the old man seemed. Now was the time. The moment when one generation presses the baton into younger, stronger fists. And if that earlier generation resented handing it on, then he should reach out and snatch it.

A duty, not a right.

'I'll look after things from now, Pa,' he said, bending forward and breathing boozy fumes into his father's face 'You should rest. Jaz can take you home. Sleep in your own bed. I'll have someone fetch you back tomorrow morning when everything's sorted.'

Joginder looked as though he had been struck. He slowly shook his head in hurt disbelief. Jaz, sitting nearby, ran over, glared daggers at her brother and reached for her father's hand but he snatched it away, looking at her as though seeing a stranger. For a ghastly moment, Gurinder thought his father was going to cry, but then Joginder's face darkened and he shook his head more vigorously.

'Pa...' Gurinder began, feeling for a path back from the precipice he now realised he was looking over.

'Who do you think you're talking to?' Joginder shouted, his face now contorted with fury. He rocked back and forth in frustration, enraged that he couldn't stand square and stare down his foolish, drunken son. Gurinder glanced around with an embarrassed smile on his face as his father's rage dissolved into a fit of coughing. He was uncomfortably aware that by now several people were following the escalating row, though all studiously avoided looking towards him and pretended, not very convincingly, not to be listening. 'I'll decide who goes and who stays,' croaked Joginder, more calmly and with absolute clarity. 'Not you. Me. *Kwisha? Bas.*'

'Everything OK, Uncle?' asked Satnam, automatically heading to Joginder's side at the sound of raised voices.

Gurinder, stung and shamed by his father's dismissal, turned on Satnam, his nose an inch from his face. 'Bugger off,' he spat, 'This has fuck-all to do with you.'

Joginder, the matter now closed, sniffed moistly and picked up his box of tissues. 'Empty,' he muttered. 'Go and buy me some more,' he told Jaz.

'I'll go with her,' offered Gurinder, desperate to be helpful.

'No.' said Joginder, nodding across at Aruna, 'You push me over to her.'

VII

'You again?'

'Me again.' Joginder smiled. 'Are you sure there's nothing you need? Would you like me to have someone take you back through to the main terminal? Get you something?'

Aruna glanced down at the urn on her lap. 'We're as well off here as out there.' She paused, then looked up, eyes narrowed. 'And I don't need looking after, thank you very much. You don't need to add me to your brood. I look terrible in yellow. You concentrate on getting your son married.'

'It's not my son. The one who just pushed me over is my son, God help me.'

She gave him a long, cool look.

'Sorry. It's the son of an old friend that's getting wed. I was with his father when . . . Well, best not to think about it now. See the boy in the grey jacket over there?' he said, pointing to Satnam, sitting alone, finishing off the last of his stash of Marmite sandwiches.

'The dark one?' She screwed up her eyes to focus, then wrinkled up her nose. 'Is he eating beef?'

'It's not beef,' sighed Joginder, wishing he had a pound for every time he'd had this conversation.

'I can smell it from here.'

'Maybe you can. But it's still not beef. Bovril is beef. That's Marmite. Marmite is yeast extract.'

'It smells like beef to me.'

'It smells like shit to me, *behenji*, but that doesn't mean it is,' he snapped, exasperated. 'I'm sorry. Excuse my language. See the girl he's talking to now?' he asked, more calmly. 'She's my daughter.'

Jaz had paused in front of Satnam on her way to buy the tissues. She made an exaggerated performance of waving away the smell of his sandwiches which made them both laugh.

The chill seemed to be affecting her particularly badly. She was shuddering. He unbuttoned his jacket, slipped it off and without a word draped it around her hunched shoulders.

'You should watch those two,' Aruna warned.

'Rubbish,' sniffed Joginder. 'They're like brother and sister.'

She offered him a tissue, which he refused, then accepted.

'They don't look like it to me.' She said.

'That's because you are a very silly old woman.'

'And you are a very rude and short-sighted old man.'

Alex and Khadija shared a Marathon bar and a can of Sprite.

'We carry on?' she asked, suddenly.

Alex nodded, brushing a sprinkling of chocolate off his jacket. 'Of course.'

'I just wondered . . .'

'What?'

'Nothing.' She stood up and straightened her clothes. 'I wish I'd put a change of underwear in our hand luggage. I suppose all the stuff we packed for . . . the baby is in Paris by now. What are you smiling at?'

'Our bags are having a better trip than we are. We should ring Uncle Duncan to make sure he got home OK.'

Khadija nodded. 'You do it. It'll mean more to him if you call. Tell him to check in the workshop. I've left his presents there.'

Alex smiled, leaned forward and took her hand. 'You think of everything. What did we get him?'

'A bottle of Dalwhinnie and a pair of slippers.'

VIII

Satnam sat next to Bhao Shinde on the single bench of three seats near the snack bar, watching Jaz as she purchased four small packs of tissues. Balraj Sopal said something to her, which she pointedly ignored. Tegbir, who had clearly caught whatever it was he said, glanced across at Satnam, whispered something and sniggered. Satnam debated going over to talk to them, warn them to watch their mouths around Jaz, but couldn't be bothered. They were wankers. Everyone knew that. But they were harmless. Everybody knew that too.

'Nice girl, is she?' Bhao asked.

Satnam shrugged. 'Yeah. Amazing backhand.'

'Your future wife?'

'Oh, her. No. She doesn't play badminton. She's great in other ways though,' Satnam added hurriedly. 'She's kind. Has a great sense of humour. Everyone likes her. Why?'

'You didn't seem too upset when the flight left without us,' Bhao observed. 'I notice these things. When everyone else was shouting and beating their breasts, you and I smiled. Now, why would that be?'

Satnam leaned forward, his elbows on his knees, still focused on Jaz, who had just said something to Balraj that made Tegbir laugh at his expense. 'It's complicated.'

'Well, we're not going anywhere.'

'Suppose when we get married we find we hate each other?'

'You won't. I can promise you that. At least, not at first. Hate, at the risk of being simplistic, is like a good curry. It takes effort, time and masala. Small quantities maybe: a pinch of indifference and a dash of contempt, but each seasons, blends in and plays its part whilst the main ingredients, the great betrayals and major failings, they need to be left to marinate over time. In twenty years' time you may hate each other, in fact you probably will, but not next week, next month or next year. So why worry? You could both be long gone before that.'

'I'm guessing you don't make your living as a marriage guidance counsellor?'

'No, 'replied Bhao seriously. 'But I suspect I would have been pretty good at it if I had.'

'And you've never been married?'

'Ah, now there you would be wrong. I was married once, a long time ago. A lovely girl. Good family. The best.'

'But?'

'But it didn't last. We've been apart for years now, but when I get home, who knows? Maybe we'll get back together. We never came to hate each other though. Never did, and I doubt now we ever will. Of course we were from the same place. Spoke the same language.'

'So do we.'

'Do you? I bet your future wife's family say you speak like foreigners. Act like outsiders. Live like Angrez.'

'Thanks. So what about you?'

'What about me?'

'You said you smiled too when we heard we couldn't go. So why was that?'

'Because I like it here. India is my one true home, always will be, but I want to stay here a little while longer.'

'Then why don't you?'

'Because it's not up to me any more. Anyway, you shouldn't worry. I'm sure you'll be fine.'

'Maybe,' sighed Satnam, unconvinced. 'but what if . . . What if you love someone else?'

'Do you?'

'I don't know. But just suppose?'

'Then, as you earlier observed, that's complicated.'

Alex dialled Uncle Duncan's number three times. Each time listened to it ring over and over, imagining the old man fast asleep in front of the log burner or out feeding his chicken and his beloved peacock. He gave up, promising himself he'd try again later.

IX

Through the long evening the tone with which the airline staff spoke to the remaining passengers steadily changed. From coolly detached, they became increasingly hostile. Vouchers were still issued with monotonous regularity, but requests for information or even simple attempts at engagement were met with snapped, aggressive dismissal. At eight the snack bar closed after its most profitable day on record. The men who had passed the day drinking around it returned to the main seating area and sat, arms folded, sullen and grumpy until someone suggested opening the bottles of duty-free alcohol they had, to a man, earlier purchased.

As the first seal cracked, a particularly officious desk clerk stood up, waving an admonishing finger. 'You can't open those bottles here. Not until you are out of the country. Put them away or I'll call the police.'

Several people stretched out on benches, arms folded across their chests. That too was promptly forbidden. Finally, at ten to ten, the staff announced that they would shortly be going off duty and closing the lounge. At that point, anyone remaining would no longer be the responsibility of the airline but would be trespassing and liable to arrest. This, they were assured, really was their very last chance.

For Balraj Sopal, for whom run-ins with the police had been part of is coming of age, this was a pretty hollow threat. Tegbir, however, with outstanding matters pending before West London Magistrates' Court, was somewhat more pensive. And for the first time, Joginder's and Khadija's views diverged.

'We have to stay,' Khadija urged. 'Otherwise all the time we've already spent here will have been wasted.'

'We should go,' said Joginder. 'If we get arrested we stand to lose a lot more than a flight to Bombay.'

'Uh, uh!' said Khadija, shaking her head. 'That's just what they're relying on us thinking. Poor, scared Asians who never kick up a fuss. Well, that's not the way it is. We're British citizens. They think they can frighten us with threats they'd never dare make to whites? No one's going to arrest anyone,' Khadija assured him. 'They're just trying to scare us. That's all.'

'Well, it's working on me,' said Alex, loyally by her side. 'And I am white. Does it seem to be getting colder in here?'

It was. The heating had been discreetly switched off half an hour earlier and a distinct chill could now be felt. Coats, gloves, hats and scarves were donned and people huddled closer together. Khadija wrapped her scarf around her neck, hunched her shoulders, folded her arms across her chest and said, simply, 'We're staying.' She looked hard at Joginder, then reached out for Alex's gloved hand.

Joginder nodded thoughtfully as he looked around his family. His tired, unhappy, uncertain family. He saw two of his nephews, sulking over some squabble, slumped on a bench, studiously ignoring one another. Satnam, over by the snack bar, sitting arms folded and legs apart, so solid and reliable he looked like he'd put down roots. Jaz, sitting alone, again with that secret smile. All looking back at him to decide for them what was right. He looked at Aruna, who met his stare and nodded imperceptibly. Only Gurinder, still smarting from the loss of face he had suffered, wouldn't meet his gaze.

Joginder put out his hand to Khadija. '*Acha.* We all stay,' he said. 'I hope you know what you are doing.'

Khadija smiled down at him and shook the offered hand. 'What *we* are doing,' she corrected him.

X

The airline staff, cocooned in thick greatcoats with wide collars turned up, raised gloved hands in a silent, unfriendly farewell and switched off the lights. The lounge was now lit only by the glow from the illuminated roadways and runways outside. The revolving beam atop a stationary snowplough slopped orange light back and forth. Long, distorted shadows were cast. Everything looked very foreign and more than a little scary. Once more people stretched out on benches, but now they curled up quiet, like abandoned children, wrapped in anything and everything they could find to wear in their hand luggage. Discarded newspapers were reclaimed, carefully smoothed out to double as thin blankets. The lounge resembled a temporary shelter for the displaced and the homeless as they settled uncomfortably, with more than an occasional fearful glance at the now dark and menacingly silent passageways, to await the arrival of the police.

Having polished off snacks packed for the journey or bought from the kiosk hours ago, cold and hungry people started to pick through the edible presents they carried in their hand luggage. Callard & Bowser Nougat. Cadbury's Fruit & Nut bars. Bags of sugared almonds, Chocolate Brazils and cardboard tubes of Famous Names liqueurs. Whereas earlier bitings had been pooled and shared, these were consumed within furtive, suspicious little cliques.

Jaz shuffled along the bench, up closer to Satnam.

Alex and Khadija, still holding hands, toyed with separate and unshared thoughts about their potential child, awaiting them in Bombay.

Joginder frowned at his son Gurinder, sitting with Balraj and Tegbir, sipping whisky, eating Toblerone chocolate and glowering at Satnam.

Aruna mourned her dead son. The smell of his hair when wet. The taste of his tears when young. The heat of his pain in death.

Out beyond Gate 8 nothing moved. Across the airfield, no one ventured. Even the snow had stopped falling and the fog had now lifted.

The night was crystal bright and the over-lit vista of concrete, tarmac and asphalt resembled a film set readied for some vast and spectacular disaster epic. The snow-covered planes looked artificial. Unreal and frail. Hollow fibreglass and flimsy balsa wood mock-ups.

Bhao turned from this chill vista with a grim smile.

'And now,' he observed, to no one in particular, 'the fun starts.'

ACT III

I

With food to be delivered to cut-off communities, old folk living alone to be fetched in to hastily prepared centres, stranded motorists to be rescued and distant accidents to be managed the severely overstretched police gave as little priority to a peaceful sit-in by a group of airline passengers as the media had. As the minutes ticked away and the approach of legal authority and lawful retribution failed to materialise, so confidence progressively returned. Many found they couldn't sleep and murmured conversation could once more be heard.

'I'm just saying, it's not right,' Balraj said once more. Tegbir agreed.

Gurinder reached for the bottle of whisky. Shook it, setting the amber liquid slopping around inside the near empty bottle. He belched, grimaced at the bitter taste of bile rising, belched again and handed the bottle on.

Satnam and Jaz stared out across the airport. Jaz removed an earring. Satnam smiled. 'What?' she asked, smiling back, her head to one side.

Balraj took a long pull. 'Fuck! Look at him,' he said, nodding towards Satnam. 'Who the fuck does he think he is? I'm telling you man, if it was my sister he was sniffing around . . .'

Gurinder shook his aching head. 'You're talking bollocks. You always do. I should never have listened to you. Oh God, I think I'm gonna throw up.'

'I was thinking about when you got your ears pierced,' Satnam said. 'Remember?'

'I'm hardly likely to forget it.'

'You, and who was it? Bini, Rom, Bal?'

'And those girls from Number 23. Remember them?'

'Oh, yeah.'

'Your mum with the needle and thread and half a potato. Us all lined up, terrified.'

'*Don't worry, beti. It doesn't hurt,*' mimicked Satnam.

'Well, it did. And pulling the thread though every day afterward. That hurt too. And you. I remember you, standing in the doorway.'

'Hmmm.'

'You cried when she did me.'

'I remember. You didn't.'

'What's going to happen to us, partner?' Jaz wondered. She frowned, drew in a breath, seemed about to say something else, but then thought better of it. She placed one finger on her lips, and beckoned Satnam to follow her. Together they wandered out past the toilets and the closed snack bar and on, out of sight of anyone at Gate 8. She took his hand and led him further still. Then, when she was absolutely sure no one could see, she stopped, let go of his hand and turned to face him.

She felt in her pocket, found her sewing kit and took out a tiny pair of scissors. She reached out, took his hand once more in hers and pushed his sleeve up to reveal the *rakhi* that she had tied on him four months earlier. Then, it had been brightly coloured, neatly plaited and twisted through with gold and deep red tinsel thread. Now it hung thin, loose and faded. Slipping a finger between the *rakhi* and his wrist, she snipped through the thread.

'I don't want to be your sister any more, Rocky', she said, quietly.

'Why not?'

'This is why not.' Leaning forward on tiptoe, her hand still resting on his, she kissed him.

He pulled back, glanced nervously around, frowned, smiled, half laughed, and gently, thoughtfully, reached out to touch her cheek. 'This . . .'

Her eyes filled with tears. 'Complicates things. I know. But I can't let you get married without knowing there's an alternative, and it's me.'

II

Alex sat with Khadija's head on his lap. He lightly stroked her hair as he watched her sleep, marvelling as always at her ability to just switch off and her absolute stillness in repose. It was hard even to detect a breath.

When they were first married, her utter stillness when asleep used to scare him: he would convince himself she had died in her sleep. He would get so perturbed he'd end up waking her, and his sheer joy in her being alive made her smile.

At moments like this he still couldn't believe she had finally agreed to marry him. Quite why remained for him one of life's greatest and most glorious mysteries. He returned to his book but the light was too poor to read comfortably and anyway, he couldn't concentrate. He felt dreadfully tired, and shivered, feeling terribly cold, deep inside. Very gently, so as not to disturb her, he eased his copy of the photograph of their prospective child from his pocket and looked at it.

A short distance away, but near enough so that he could hear her laboured breathing, Aruna nodded. Near to sleep, she muttered something, a name perhaps, but what it was he didn't quite hear.

'With the benefit of hindsight,' Bhao observed, watching Alex's shuddering, 'more to eat might have been a better idea. Alcohol lowers the body temperature.' He paused. 'You or her?'

'What?'

'Is it you or is it her? I imagine you are going to adopt that child because you can't have one of your own. But we both know couples aren't just childless. One or the other is infertile. Sterile. Like snow? I was just wondering if it was you or if it was her?'

'I'm sorry but...'

'Is it any of my business? None at all.'

'I was going to say, does it matter?'

'Not to me it doesn't. I imagine it matters mightily to you. Or of course, to her. But I suspect it's you.'

'What gives you the right . . .' began Alex, but then he stopped and let out a long, shaky breath. 'Of course it matters. And you're right. It is me, as it happens.'

Bhao sat down beside Alex. 'You know what happened to me as I walked back from the surgery the day I got the test results? The ones that confirmed I'd have to make this journey?' he asked, speaking very quietly. 'There I was, walking along, deep in thought and a blackbird, all ripped up and bloody, its eyes pecked out, hopped and flapped across my path. The screaming flock of crows that had torn it up, its winged lynch mob, wheeled off and promptly turned on me! I heard a screech, glanced round and was eyeball to eyeball with a gape-beaked crow, blood up, screaming and angry. As I ducked, and tried to shoo it away, so another dived and tore at my ear. A third swooped at my forehead. Why was that, I wonder? How long ago did you hear?'

Alex blew out his cheeks, then let the air escape in a slow, silent whistle. 'A year, just over. Of course, we couldn't leave it at that. Oh no.' He glanced down at Khadija, his mouth twisted as though the words tasted sour. 'People like us don't accept the inevitability of bad things happening. We don't resign ourselves to misfortune. Not us. We protest and we resist. Challenge, negotiate, persuade and overcome or, if all that fails, we circumvent. First there were more tests. Then a biopsy. And if you think this has been a bit of a low point, try laying in a clinic, nauseous from an anaesthetic, aching like you've had a good kicking whilst some twerp in a white coat assures you that your balls are among the poorest he's ever seen, knowing you've paid several hundred pounds for the thumbs down. Let me tell you even wanking off to order in a chilly clinic pales in comparison.'

Bhao laughed, and to his own surprise, Alex did too. He felt tears on his face and, embarrassed, he wiped them away with the heel of his palm.

'So once convinced you couldn't be a father...'

'I can be a father. I just can't produce sperm.'

'Accepted. So?'

'We decided to adopt.'

'From India.'

Alex nodded. 'My wife's cousin suggested it. Said it would be better.'

'Better in what way?'

'So the baby can be an Indian, like my wife.'

'Hmm. An Indian. Is she really?'

'Of course.'

'A country in which she's never lived, of which I imagine neither of you hold citizenship and to which you now go only to find and take away a child? You're like those Sikhs going to India to get a bride because it's their home. An interesting concept of a home.'

'It's where they come from. Where she comes from.'

'How much of what's wrong with the world is encapsulated in that simple phrase? The poisonous myth of the eternal homeland. When did any of your wife's family last reside in India? When did one of those Sopals? Fifty years ago? Hundred years ago?'

Khadija stirred, and Alex turned to her, laying a hand lightly on her shoulder. Her slight frown faded and she stretched and opened one eye. 'Who are you talking to?' she asked sleepily.

Alex looked around, but Bhao, as seemed to be his wont, had once more drifted off.

'No one,' he said, quietly. 'Myself, I guess.' He shifted slightly, and Khadija raised her head. Carefully he moved out from beneath her. 'Sorry,' he said. 'I need the loo.'

'Did you get through to Uncle Duncan?'

Alex shook his head. 'It's too late to try now. I'll try him again in the morning.'

III

Satnam and Jaz lurked near the toilets like nervous conspirators, suddenly embarrassed to be so close together, yet scared to be apart. She still wore his grey jacket, ludicrously big, draped over her shoulders. They leapt away from one another and stood, artificially relaxed, as Alex passed, nodding to them. Jaz smiled back at him.

'We need to talk to my father,' she whispered to Satnam.

'Oh God,' groaned Satnam. 'Are you crazy? What am I going to say?'

'Tell him. Say we're not going to India. Tell him the wedding's off.' Her eyes narrowed. 'You don't still want to get married, do you?'

'No, Jaz. I never wanted to get married. Unless,' he added, looking at the floor. 'I get married to you.'

She took his arm, shivered and squeezed up close to him.

'What the fuck . . .?'

It was Gurinder, staggering, bleary-eyed, towards the urinals.

'Satnam and me. We . . .' began Jaz.

'Have you been messing with my sister?' he roared at Satnam, completely ignoring her. 'Is that what all this badminton shit has been about? You two at it in the back of the van. Is that it?'

Jaz stepped towards him. Rested a hand on his arm, 'Please, Gur,' she said, but he shook her off.

'Don't touch me, *randi!*' Gurinder shouted. All his failed enterprises, his doomed attempts to gain respect. All the slights and the sneers he'd ever received. Every shitty, unfair thing that had ever happened to him boiled down to this. A sister's betrayal and this outsider's abuse of trust.

Balraj and Tegbir, sucked towards trouble as crows are drawn to carrion, slunk over, hands in pockets and smirks on faces. Gurinder turned to them, trembling with fury. 'You were right. You were fucking right! This darky bastard has been banging my sister!'

Satnam looked around, hoping to spot and appeal to Joginder to intercede but his three cousins squared up to him and blocked his line of sight. He was not frightened, nor, as yet, was he angry, though he glowered at Gurinder for foul-mouthing Jaz.

Gurinder nodded towards the toilets. 'In there.'

Satnam shook his head. 'You are kidding?' he asked, still not quite able to take this situation seriously.

'Stop it,' cried Jaz, more conscious of the viciousness her brother was capable of than Satnam, and thus much more scared. 'This is crazy. Please, Gurinder, don't.'

'Shut up, *randi!*' snapped Gurinder.

'Make that the last time you call her that,' warned Satnam.

'I'll call her whatever the fuck I like, *kalia,*' spat Gurinder. Jaz made a break for her father, but Gurinder grabbed her arm before she could get past them. He pushed her into Balraj's embrace. 'Keep hold of her. And keep her quiet.' Balraj happily grabbed her, feigning indifference to where his hands were actually placed. With a threatening bellow, Satnam threw himself at the leering Balraj, but was knocked off balance by a vicious kick behind the knee which folded his leg and sent him stumbling. Gurinder and Tegbir grabbed him. Jaz shouted.

'Shut her up!' snarled Gurinder. He and Tegbir used Satnam's momentum to push him into and through the door marked Gents. Balraj crushed his hand hard down over Jaz's mouth and dragged her away, wondering why she'd suddenly gone so limp.

Their momentum carried Gurinder, Tegbir and Satnam into the toilets, across the tiled floor, and up hard against the washbasins. Alex, still zipping up his flies, leapt back, stunned and scared as they crashed in through the door, which slammed back against the wall and swung twisted on its hinges, half closing behind them. Satnam's yellow turban tumbled across the floor as his face was forced up against the mirror above the sinks. Gurinder, leaning in on him from behind to keep him bent over the basins, repeatedly hit him in the kidneys. 'Fuck off, *gora,*' he panted at Alex, jerking his head towards the door. 'Out.'

Alex, his back pressed against the far wall, edged past the battling Sikhs, knowing he should do something but too shocked, confused and just plain terrified to be able to think what that might be. Tegbir thrust his knee up hard at Satnam's stomach and groin, over and over, whilst aiming crazed punches at his head.

The blows raining in and down on him, delivered with huge grunts of effort and much cursing, did less damage to Satnam than might have been expected. Most landed wide of their mark. Unlike Satnam, who knew how to apply violence with economy and efficiency, the men setting about him were at best noisy roughhouse brawlers. Big on the verbals and posturing but too wide-swinging, showy and pumped up when actually called upon to slug it out to do really cruel damage, unless random chance intervened. At one point, Tegbir had to haul off, swearing furiously and shaking his hand in agony, having completely missed the side of Satnam's head and connected instead with the cold tap on the sink.

That was how random chance intervened.

Satnam, sensing in Tegbir's agonised wail a shift in the odds and the opportunity he had been waiting for, jerked himself upright, placed both hands on the rim of the sink and pushed back against Gurinder's weight. Unfortunately, this move not only coincided with Tegbir's return to the fray with a renewed attempt to knee him but also positioned Satnam to receive the blow square in his unprotected belly. Totally winded, he doubled over in pain, his face smashing down into the tap Tegbir had just hit. Blood flooded into his mouth and exploded from his burst nose as he desperately tried to draw in breath. He choked, coughed, gasped and spat out blood and saliva. Gurinder grabbed his hair, pulled his head back then crashed it down onto the rim of the ceramic sink. Satnam went limp and slid, semi-conscious, to the floor.

Gurinder wiped the back of his hand across his mouth, stepped back and aimed a last, vicious kick at Satnam's head. Fists were now pounding on the toilet door — against which Tegbir leaned, cradling his damaged hand — drawing their attention away from their comatose victim and towards the urgent need for flight.

IV

Alex had run first to Khadija. Trembling, he told her in a garbled rush all he had just witnessed. Together they found Joginder, with whom Alex returned to the toilets. Khadija went off alone to find and alert Jaz, unaware that she was quite literally being held by Balraj.

Joginder's face, set once again in a warder's glower, could have been hacked from stone. Stamped out of metal. No thoughts or emotions showed. By the time they reached the toilet, Satnam's attackers were long gone. Alex pushed open the door and tried unsuccessfully to negotiate Joginder's chair through it. The floor was slippery, bespattered with bloody water. The wall-mounted roll of towelling had been dislodged and hung now at a crazy angle, its loop of blue cloth twisted and ripped. A broken tap gushed water into a cracked, blood-smeared basin. Satnam lay, flat out and face down, his head half under the pipe work beneath the line of sinks, his breathing heavy, wet, snorting and pained. His face was covered with blood which bubbled around his mouth. Joginder gulped down a sob, half swore and part prayed, thoughts wrapped around one another at the point where oath, blasphemy and plea all become one.

And it was blindingly clear there was no way his chair was going through the doorway. At least not with an inexperienced and deeply frightened handler like Alex shoving and hauling at it. 'Leave me,' Joginder said, impatiently, his chair jammed halfway through the door. 'Go. Get him into the recovery position.'

Under Joginder's direction Alex heaved Satnam over onto his side. Following curtly issued instructions, he folded the comatose Sikh's large arms, bent his legs, raised his chin. Looking up to Joginder for further orders, he saw tears of impotent torment in the older man's eyes. As Alex watched, Joginder slowly raised himself, inch by inch, his hands forcing down on the arms of his chair, his whole body shaking with the effort. He leaned forward and fell towards the line of sinks, grabbing at them for support, his useless legs trailing behind him. Agonisingly slowly, hand over hand, he dragged himself towards where Satnam lay.

Alex reached out help him. 'Leave me alone!' Joginder snarled, his voice harsh and rasping through the exertion. In spite of the cold, sweat soaked his clothes and ran into his eyes. 'Go. Get help. Find a doctor. Go!'

The moment Alex left, Joginder let himself slide to the floor. Once on the ground, and with a mighty effort, he hauled himself over to fetch up next to the still unconscious Satnam. He propped himself up onto one elbow, shuffling his useless lower limbs around until he could reach out and touch Satnam's bruised and bloody head. He murmured to him. Broken, simple, old words. '*Bas. Kwisha. Bas.*'

V

Alex half fell into the area around Gate 8. He cast a quick glance around for Khadija, then: 'There's been . . . are any of you a doctor?' he panted, bending over to catch his breath.

Given the legion of medicos then keeping the National Health Service going across the UK who had learnt their skills in India, it was statistically quite likely there would be at least one. In fact, there were two. Ali Masood and Ashvini Majumdar.

Both rose, then, spotting the other, promptly sat back down again. Both had been waiting, resigned and increasingly resentful, for just this call. Young men, drinking all day, stressed, dehydrated and overtired? They would have taken bets. Offered odds. And both had more than enough experience to be pretty sure that whatever had happened, it would turn out to be petty, messy and thoroughly unpleasant.

'There's blood everywhere,' pleaded Alex. 'He really needs a doctor. Please.'

The two doctors introduced themselves to one another, quickly summarising their backgrounds and current status. He, a general practitioner with a surgery on a depressed council estate outside Dundee, she much more recently qualified and for the past eighteen months a registrar in Milton Keynes General.

'I guess that makes you senior,' said Dr Majumdar, thinking this a strong argument for him being the one to go.

'True,' nodded Dr Masood, clearly of the view it argued precisely the opposite.

'I haven't got any equipment,' Dr Masood pointed out, his reasonable smile starting to wear thin and his professional tone developing a certain edge.

'And I do?' asked Dr Majumdar, an eyebrow raised. He was going to have to do a great deal better than that.

'No. But you do have much more up to date A and E experience.'

'I really think it might need you both,' said Alex, desperately.

They both got up. 'Oh, very well,' grumbled Dr Masood, patting his pockets to make sure he had his glasses ready to hand. 'Coming?'

'By all means,' smiled Dr Majumdar, turning to Alex. 'Lead the way.'

In the toilet, Bhao eased himself down onto the floor next to Joginder. The older man still held Satnam's head. Satnam's breathing was still laboured and his eyes closed.

'I should have seen this coming,' sighed Joginder. 'It's like that old woman said. She could see it. Even Gurinder could see what I failed to, or didn't want to. See that he and my daughter were...'

'What? Fond of each other? In love? Screwing around? Do you really think that justifies what your son's done here? Let me guess, in a moment you're going to talk about honour and your family's good name. You know, you remind me of that joke about a tribe of pygmies called the Fuquawe because they wander through the long grass, leaping into the air every so often shouting, 'Where the fuck are we?' Except in your case, it's *who* the fuck are we? People call you Pakis, but not one of you is from Pakistan. Your passports may call you British but you don't think you are and nor does anyone else. You call yourselves Indians, but we don't. It's time to make a choice, or you'll be foreigners everywhere and forever. Fake as the fashions you make.'

'What gives you the right to talk to me, to any of us, like this?'

'You do.'

Joginder moaned, low and pained. 'Everything I've tried to do. All I've tried to be.'

'You really think this is at all about you?' asked Bhao.

'It's all finally falling apart,' concluded Joginder as Alex entered with the two doctors.

'Perhaps,' said Bhao, leaving. 'Or perhaps it's all finally coming together.'

VI

As the first hint of a false dawn briefly lit the sky, Khadija wandered ever farther from Gate 8, calling for Jaz. From a darkened corner she heard grunting, sobbing, and a female voice, stressed and breathless, called back to her. Sick now with fear for Jaz, Khadija ran shouting for help towards her voice, turned a corner and came to a sudden, horrified halt, stunned by the sight that awaited her.

Balraj lay curled on the floor, foetal and whimpering, cradling his scrotum. Jaz stood a few paces away, bending, stretching and seemingly doing a full warm up, as though preparing for a match, or warming down after a session in a gym.

'Wow! Now that's not a routine much favoured by Torvill and Dean,' Khadija said.

Jaz looked up, swept back her hair from her face, her mouth a thin, determined line. She did two quick neck rolls. 'Yeah? Well, they're not Sopals. They're not even Sikhs.'

'Look,' began Khadija. Your partner . . .'

'Satnam? Shit! What have they done to him? Where is he?'

In her rage Jaz had channelled all thoughts and emotions on remembering and applying the skills she had learnt on a 'Self Defence for Asian Girls' course the local police had run following a series of attacks three years earlier. Successfully. Balraj was now not only the distressed possessor of two severely bruised testicles, but also a dislocated thumb, a swollen throat and a left shin virtually stripped of skin. Jaz was still in two minds about her decision to leave him with both eyes intact.

'Take me to him,' Jaz said, after deciding one final knee drop onto her cousin's midriff wouldn't go amiss.

Dr Majumdar knelt beside Satnam whilst Alex and Dr Masood got Joginder back into his wheelchair. Having ensured his airways were clear of any obstructions, she checked pulse at wrist and neck, lifted an eyelid to gauge pupil dilation then gently felt around Satnam's neck, scalp and face, quietly asking him if he could hear her, what he could feel and where it hurt most. Dr Masood snatched handfuls of toilet paper, bunched them up and soaked them in cold water. As he did so he bombarded Joginder and Alex with questions: Did they know how many times had Satnam been hit? Where? By how many people was he attacked? How long ago did it happen? How long had he been out? Was he on any medication? Did he have a history of epilepsy? Together the two doctors cleaned him up, stretched him out from the recovery position, without a moment's thought stripping off their jackets, His to be bundled up to make a pillow for Satnam's head, her long coat to serve as a blanket.

They looked at one another, conferred briefly, then Dr Masood rose, turned and pointed to the door.

'I watched his father die,' said Joginder. 'All because I wasn't quick enough to see what was going on around us. I won't let that happen again. Whatever it takes. However much it costs, put this right.'

And most painful, expensive beyond imagining, he whispered, 'Please.'

Ali Masood smiled. 'Relax. It looks a lot worse than it probably is. Maxillofacial injuries usually do. He's clearly been through hell and may well be a bit shaky for a day or two but apart from a broken nose it looks like mainly cuts and bruises. Just to be on the safe side though we ought to get him to hospital. I'm assuming someone's already called the police?'

Khadija and Jaz ran up. Jaz pushed through to get into the toilet but Ali stopped her, an arm across the doorway.

'Not just yet,' he said gently, detached, kind and professional but very clear who was in charge. 'You can see him in a minute or two.'

She turned and threw herself into her father's arms, racked with sobbing so wholehearted as he stroked her hair and murmured 'Bas' that Khadija found it difficult to reconcile this bereft child with the vengeful harridan that had visited such brutal retribution on Balraj moments earlier.

'There's a guy over by Gate 10 . . .' Khadija began, then faltered as Jaz turned and glared at her. The doctor sighed, raised an eyebrow, and waited. 'Forget it. It's nothing,' Khadija concluded, to his evident relief.

Ten minutes later, Jaz was with Satnam. Seeing him laying there she bunched her left hand into a fist and stuffed it up against her mouth, profoundly regretting leaving Balraj with his vision intact. Satnam tried to sit up. She dropped to his side, placed a restraining hand on his chest and eased him back.

'Do I still have to talk to your dad?' he croaked through swollen lips.

Jaz smiled. She lay down next to him. Side by side they stared up at the ceiling. 'No, Gabbar Singh, I think he's pretty much got the message.'

'Great. Let's go home.'

'Of course, there is still your mother . . .'

'Oh God,' groaned Satnam. He closed his eyes and let his head fall to one side so he was looking at her. 'Can't they just come back and hit me some more?'

VII

Walking painfully, abnormally erect, Satnam led away the departing Sopals. He had refused to have the police called. Polite, grateful but determined, he had even declined the hospital visit the two doctors had urged on him, knowing too well that difficult questions and official reports would inevitably follow.

When they had entered the airport the Sopals had resembled a briskly commanded convoy. Now, they looked more like the remnants of a collapsed and vanquished army, spirit broken, in full and abject retreat. Gone was the verve, fuss and volume and in its place was dejection, mistrust and blame. Because this was not only just a defeated force, it was one betrayed from within. That, of all thoughts, pressed down most hard on Joginder, its shamed and dismayed head.

Satnam had smiled when they had been told the previous day they would not be travelling to Bombay. He smiled again now. Before, it had been a bitter, cheerless grin. This time it was fuelled with pure joy. This time, too, it hurt. His mouth was all torn up inside and his face was swollen. It hurt like hell but still he grinned through the pain. He couldn't help it. He simply couldn't stop himself. He looked round for Jaz, saw her saying goodbye to Khadija, and the smile grew ever wider and even more painful.

Joginder had made it clear to Satnam and Jaz that he neither asked for nor expected them to show any restraint in reporting the assaults they had suffered. Made clear his view that to date only Balraj, limping, despised and ostracised, far behind the others, had received anything approaching his just desserts. None the less, he was relieved and profoundly grateful that both seemed content to leave full retribution to him and the family would be spared further public humiliation.

And dare he hope that perhaps he might at last have found a man worthy of his Jaz? Against all odds and despite some very serious complexities yet to be addressed, much closer to home than he would ever have expected?

If so, then an old debt would finally be repaid. A duty at last fulfilled.

VIII

The night sky, bruised by the dawn, purpled on the eastern horizon, erupting into angry blotches of red and dirty grey. After a few minutes, it calmed, blushed vermillion then pastelled through rose to a marbled, salmon pink. Streaks of new day were drawn ever wider and higher across the paling, vacant sky, catching and briefly setting afire the vapour trail of the first aircraft on approach. As the longest night of their lives finally drew to its end, Alex left Khadija sitting with Aruna to try, one more time, to ring Uncle Duncan. The old man was invariably up with the dawn. Alex hoped to catch him before he headed out. But when he returned to them it was obvious something was seriously wrong. Khadija rose and reached out for his hand.

'His car hit a tree, just near Cirencester,' Alex said in a small voice, his throat constricted with emotion. 'He's in hospital. I spoke to Mrs Harding from the post office. She'd just gone in to get him some things.'

'Shit! How is he?'

'She says they think he's going to be OK. Broken collarbone. Cuts. But badly shaken up and at his age...'

'We need to go home.' said Khadija, gathering up their things.

'But we can't. What about . . .'

'Alishya?' asked Khadija, unsure quite where the name had come from, but suddenly knowing it was right. That it was *all* going to be alright. 'We'll go after Christmas, or if we can't get time off then, at Easter. She's safe. Looked after. He's alone, and he's family. Let's go.'

'But there won't be buses for hours yet and the trains are all buggered up.'

'So? We're still two good earners with no kids, lover boy. Hire me a car. Call us a cab. Come on!' she smiled, squeezing his arm. 'You've got an uncle to care for. I've got a peacock to feed.'

Alex looked around the now near empty lounge in search of Bhao, wanting to say farewell but he was nowhere in sight. Gate 8 looked like the aftermath of a minor riot. The morning after a rock concert. Screwed up napkins. Shredded papers. Shards of plastic tumblers. Discarded magazines. Abandoned cartons. Scraps of stale food. Wrappers, empty packets, crushed cans, all scattered and cast across the floor. Amid this ruin, Khadija knelt beside Aruna's chair.

'Will you be OK?' she asked. 'We'll wait with you until someone comes.'

'I'll be fine,' said Aruna. 'You go. They'll take care of me. Have you named that baby yet?' she added as the first of the returning airport personnel approached.

Khadija smiled and nodded. 'Yes. As a matter of fact, I have.'

'Good. No one's real until you say their name,' she reminded Khadija.

'You're real,' Khadija smiled, 'and I've never said yours.'

'But others have. Aruna. Aruna Shinde.'

Epilogue

Less than twenty-four hours after their arrival at the airport, Alex and Khadija headed back up the airport approach road to join the sparse westbound traffic on the M4. Alex drove the rented Ford Fiesta with windows down and radio blaring to keep him alert. Khadija, with no real idea what would happen next, when they would go to Bombay, if they would adopt their child, experienced an almost euphoric sense of content as she fought a losing battle to stay awake. She felt her head nodding and her eyelids getting too heavy to hold open and knew with certainty one sure thing: that whatever her future, whatever the challenges it might hold, it would be here.

She was heading home.

It would be several days before a shamefaced Gurinder crept home, asking forgiveness and seeking reconciliation. Joginder had spent too long in prisons to believe in remorse or trust in rehabilitation. Punishment alone shrives. Only suffering purges. Such was his view. The morning after his return, Gurinder on order swapped responsibilities with Satnam and took over his driving, loading and dropping duties. Satnam worked the stall and found a thrill in bargaining neither he nor Jaz would ever have expected, whilst Balraj and Tegbir found themselves exiled to the least busy, most exposed lay-bys on the North Circular, there to hawk cut flowers, boxed mangoes and Christmas trees from the backs of rusty vans.

And the following year, Jaz and Satnam won the West London regional doubles badminton trophy.

'It's time for us to go home too,' murmured Aruna Shinde, her right hand resting lightly on the urn.

Bhao stared sadly after the others, back towards Landside, into the UK.

'I want to stay here, Ma,' he said.

'I know, son,' said Aruna, sadly. 'But we both know I have to take you home.'

'I loved you, Ma,' he said, in a voice that seemed to come from very far away.

Her eyes filled with tears. 'I know.' She breathed. 'I know.'

It was right, that it should end like this. Her, alone with his ashes, the last, dry leaf on an otherwise stripped tree, relentlessly tugged at by the buffeting winds of this hard and bitter winter. Battered, ripped and twisted, yet still stubbornly clinging on long after all the others had surrendered, tumbled and succumbed.

'Here all alone?' tutted the man who had pushed her chair the day before. 'Look,' he said, deftly flicking the brakes off with his toe and turning her chair towards the glass wall. 'See? The airport's opening up. There's the first flight fired up and ready to go. You'll get home today, dear, no doubt about it. No doubt at all.'

About the Author

Dawood Ali McCallum's novels have been published in India, Italy and the UK. His articles have appeared in journals around the world. For the past 25 years he has worked in courts, police stations and prisons in some of the world's most fragile states. He draws heavily on these experiences in his writing, as well as on extensive research in India and the UK.

Read more at https://dawoodalimccallum.com/.

www.ingramcontent.com/pod-product-compliance
Ingram Content Group UK Ltd.
Pitfield, Milton Keynes, MK11 3LW, UK
UKHW040135260225
455541UK00001B/71